PINGU

and the Messy Meal

BBC CHILDREN'S BOOKS

It was lunch-time in Pingu's house. Mum, Dad and Pingu were all sitting round the table together. Mum and Dad were tucking into a nice fresh fish.

"Eat up, Pingu," said Dad.

But Pingu was having trouble with his potatoes. Every time he tried to pick one up with his fork, it slipped off.

"Stupid fork," said Pingu and he bashed it on the table. Then it was so flat that he could get the potatoes to stay on it easily.

"Stop mucking about, Pingu," said Dad. "This is how you use your fork to eat a potato." But just as Dad raised the fork to his mouth, the potato fell off it.

Pingu hooted with laughter.

Pingu was beginning to enjoy himself and decided to blow bubbles in his glass of milk. It made a good, loud noise.

"Stop it, Pingu," warned Mum. "Just eat up your food quietly."

Pingu opened his beak as wide as he could, tipped his head back and began to dangle the fish in his throat. There was a gobbling sound and then Pingu triumphantly held up the fish skeleton to show he had eaten all the fish.

"Finished!" said Pingu and without asking he got off his chair and headed for the toybox.

"And just where do you think you're going?" said Dad. "Come straight back to the table and eat your greens."

Pingu pulled a face. "I don't like greens," he whined.

"Then I'll have to feed you like a baby," said Dad and he began to shovel forkloads of greens into Pingu's beak until Pingu felt completely full.

"Now eat that last bit up yourself," said Dad. "You want to grow into a big, strong penguin, don't you?" "I'm not sure," said Pingu in a very small voice.

There was only one thing for it. Pingu took his straw and sucked the whole lot up in one go. YUCK! thought Pingu. Now his mouth was full of greens. What was worse, no matter how hard he tried, he just couldn't swallow them.

This was an emergency. Pingu dashed to the bathroom and spat his mouthful of greens into the toilet. Then he pulled the chain.

"Bye-bye greens," he said cheerfully.

As he left the bathroom he made a face in the mirror. He was feeling rather pleased with himself.

Pingu wondered if Mum and Dad would say
anything when he came back into the room.
Did they know what he'd done?
But Mum and Dad only
watched as Pingu sidled
past them and made
a dive for his toybox.

Pingu searched through all his toys and found his ball. He wanted to play football with it but it looked very flat.

"Can you pump it up for me, please?" he asked Dad.

While Dad pumped the ball up, Pingu had a lick of Mum's ice lolly. It turned into a very large lick. "Hey!" said Mum. "That's enough!"

The ball was ready now.

"Thanks, Dad," said Pingu and he rushed off outside to play with it.

As soon as Pingu went out into the cold he needed to blow his nose. So, putting the ball down carefully on the snow, he went back inside to ask Mum for a handkerchief.

18

The minute Pingu had gone, two of his friends turned up and seized the ball.

"We can have a good game with this," they said to one another.

Inside the igloo Pingu gave his nose a big blow. "That's better," he said. "Now for some football."

But when he got back outside he found that his ball had gone.

"Thanks for asking!" he shouted angrily at his two friends when he saw them playing with it. "Give it back!"

21

The two friends didn't want to give the ball back at all.

"Come and find it," they shouted at Pingu and they ran off round the back of the igloo.

Then one of the penguins began to bounce Pingu's ball on his head over and over again.

"I hope it gives you a headache," said Pingu crossly.

23

The other penguin took over
the ball next and kicked
it forwards and
backwards over his
head with his foot.

"Show off!" shouted
Pingu.

24

At last Pingu managed to grab the ball back. He headed off home as fast as he could while his two friends pelted him with snowballs.

Then he stopped to make a face at the two penguins from between his legs and got hit – *smack* – on his bottom by a huge snowball.

Back at home Pingu told Dad what had happened.
"And now look at my ball," cried Pingu, staring
sadly at the floppy red thing on the floor. "It's gone
all flat again."

"My poor Pingu," said Mum. "Come and have a hug." And she gathered her little penguin up into her arms.

Meanwhile, Dad got out his repair kit and began to mend the ball.

"I hurt my head when I was outside, too," Pingu told Mum and he started to cry.

"Never mind," said Mum, gently. "We'll soon have you better again."

Mum put a plaster on Pingu's head . . . and Dad pumped the ball up again.

As Mum rocked Pingu in the hammock, Dad came over with something behind his back.

"Here you are, Pingu," he said and he handed Pingu his red ball. It was lovely and bouncy again.

"It's as good as new," said Dad proudly.

"Just like me!" said Pingu.

Other PINGU books available from
BBC Children's Books:

Pingu and the Birthday Present
Pingu Celebrates Christmas
Pingu the Chef
Pingu and the Circus
Pingu and the Kite
Pingu Looks After the Egg
Pingu and the Spotty Day

Pingu the Postman Wheelie Book
Pingu Lift-the-Flap Book
Pingu Address Book
Pingu Birthday Book

Fun with Pingu Activity Book
Fun with Pingu Christmas Activity Book
Fun with Pingu Colouring Book
Fun with Pingu Press-Out and Story Book
Fun with Pingu Sticker and Story Book

Pingu Mini Books
Pingu Chunky Books

Published by BBC Children's Books
a division of BBC Worldwide Limited
Woodlands, 80 Wood Lane, London W12 0TT
First published 1995
Text copyright © 1995 BBC Children's Books
Stills copyright © 1995 Editoy/SRG/BBC Worldwide
Design copyright © 1995 BBC Children's Books
Pingu copyright © 1995 Editoy/SRG/BBC Worldwide

ISBN 0 563 40393 4

Typeset by BBC Children's Books
Colour separations by DOT Gradations, Chelmsford
Printed and bound by Cambus Litho, East Kilbride